# GRAPHIC REVOLVE

If you have enjoyed this story, there are many more exciting tales for you to discover in the Graphic Revolve collection...

20,000 Leagues Under the Sea
Alice in Wonderland
Black Beauty
Dracula
Frankenstein
Gulliver's Travels
The Hound of the Baskervilles
The Hunchback of Notre Dame
King Arthur and the Knights of the Round Table
Robin Hood
The Strange Case of Dr Jekyll and Mr Hyde
Treasure Island
The War of the Worlds
The Wizard of Oz

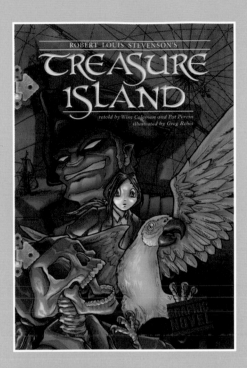

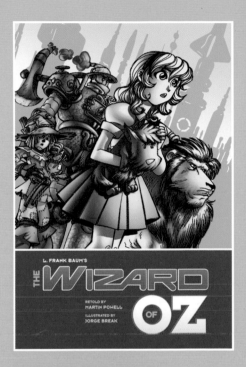

## TREASURE ISLAND

Jim Hawkins had no idea what he was getting into when the pirate Billy Bones showed up at the doorstep of his mother's inn. When Billy dies suddenly, Jim is left to unlock his old sea chest, which reveals money, a journal, and a treasure map. Joined by a band of honourable men, Jim sets sail on a dangerous voyage to locate the loot on a faraway island. The violent sea is only one of the dangers they face. They soon encounter a band of bloodthirsty pirates determined to make the treasure their own!

## THE WIZARD OF OZ

On a bright summer day, a cyclone suddenly sweeps across the Kansas sky. A young girl named Dorothy and her dog, Toto, are carried up into the terrible storm. Far, far away, they crash down in a strange land called Oz. To return home, Dorothy must travel to the Emerald City and meet the all-powerful Wizard of Oz. But the journey won't be easy, and she'll need the help of a few good friends.

# CONTENTS

SHERE KAHN

MOWGLI

CAST OF CHARACTERS

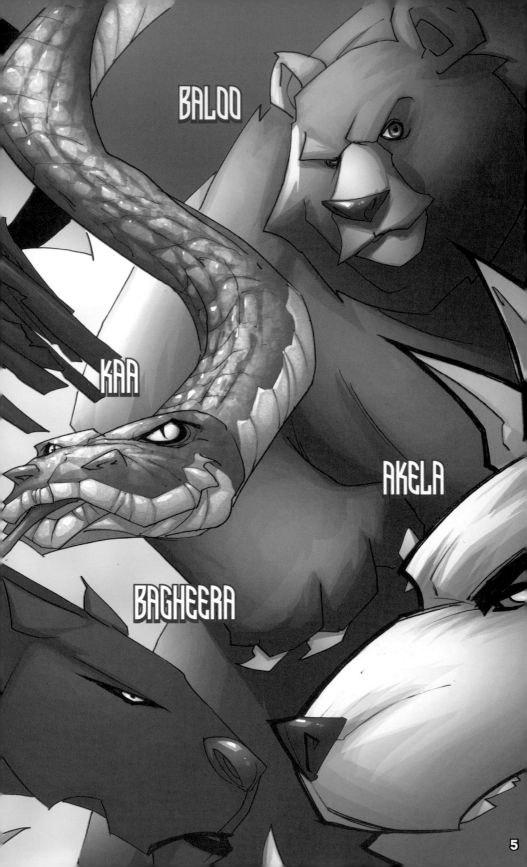

BALOO

KAA

AKELA

BAGHEERA

Many years ago, in the jungles of India . . .

# CHAPTER 1
# MOWGLI'S BROTHERS

Pheeal, Chief of the Wolves! Pheeal!

May good luck and strong teeth go with your cubs.

We have no food here, Tabaqui. What do you want?

Pheeal! Shere Khan has shifted his hunting ground.

He comes.

6

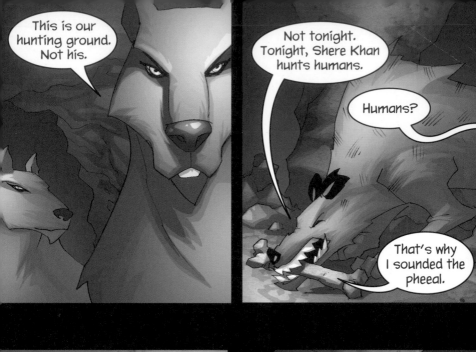

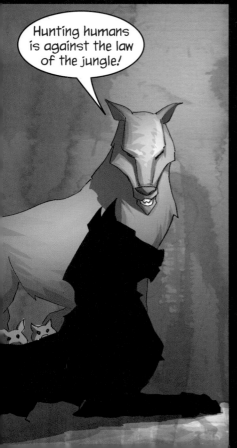

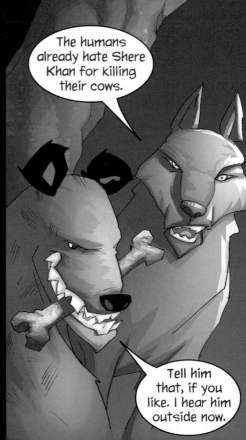

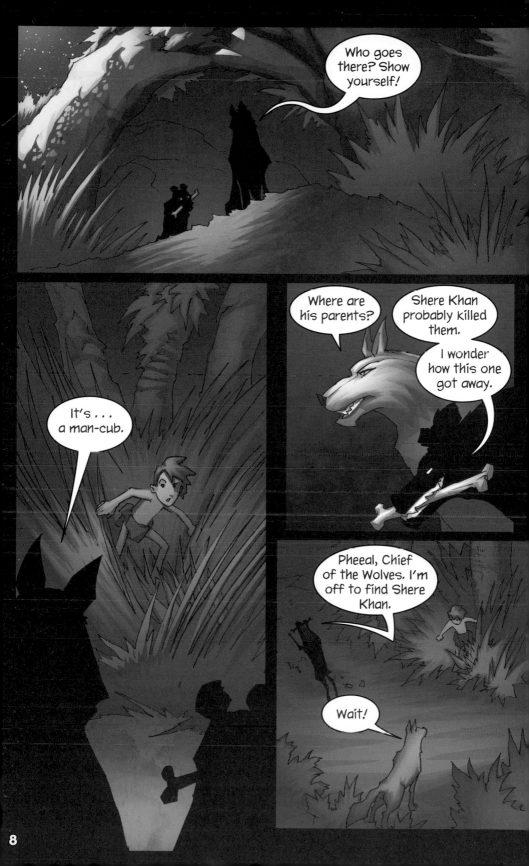

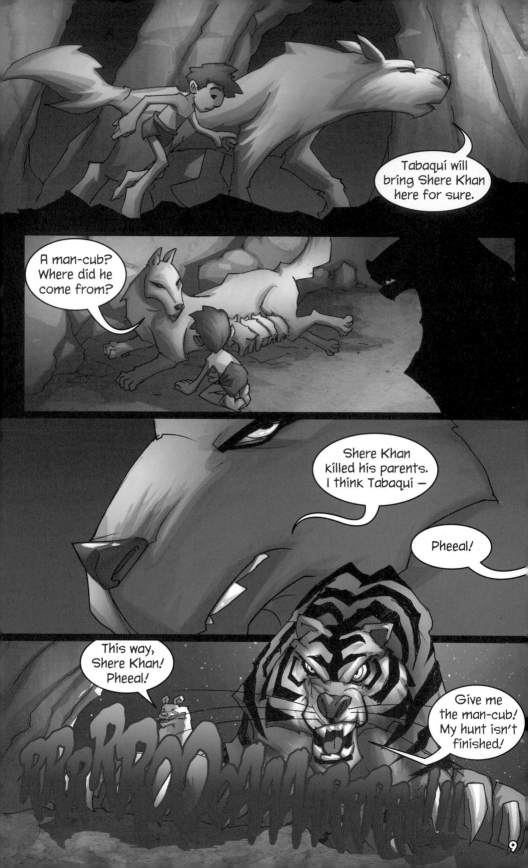

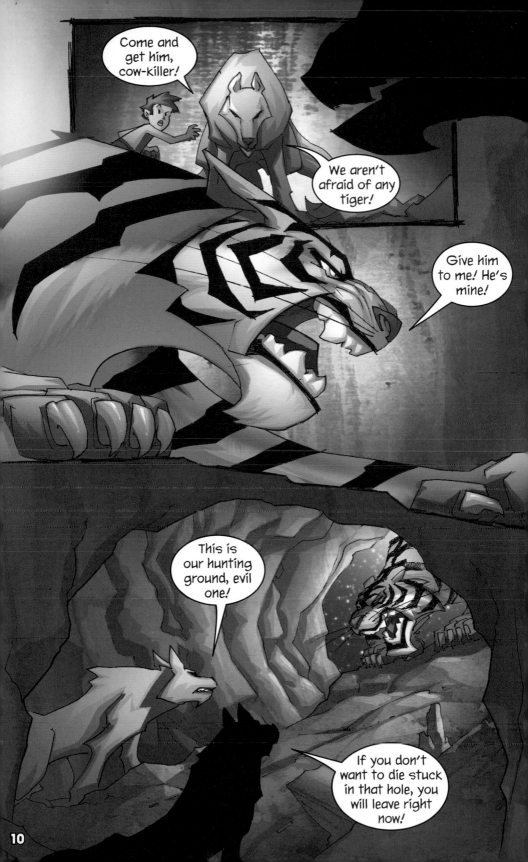

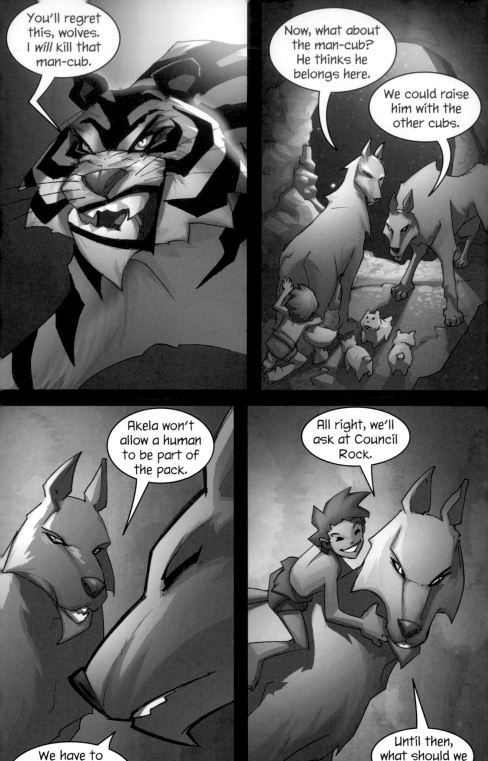

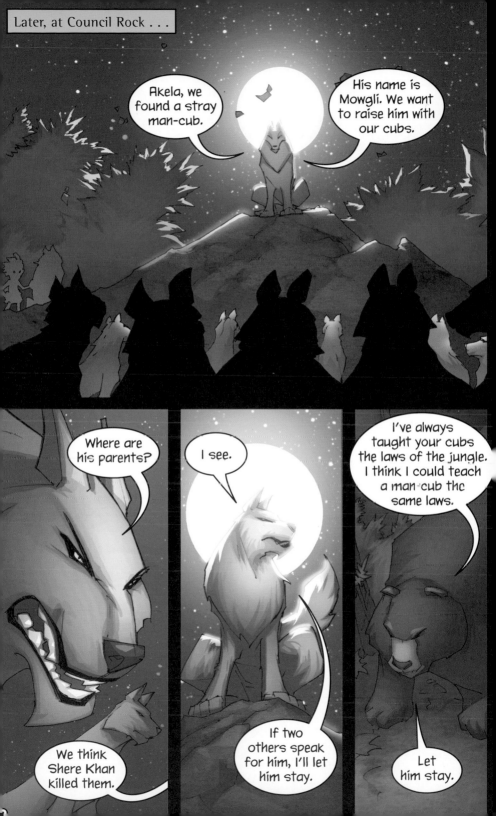

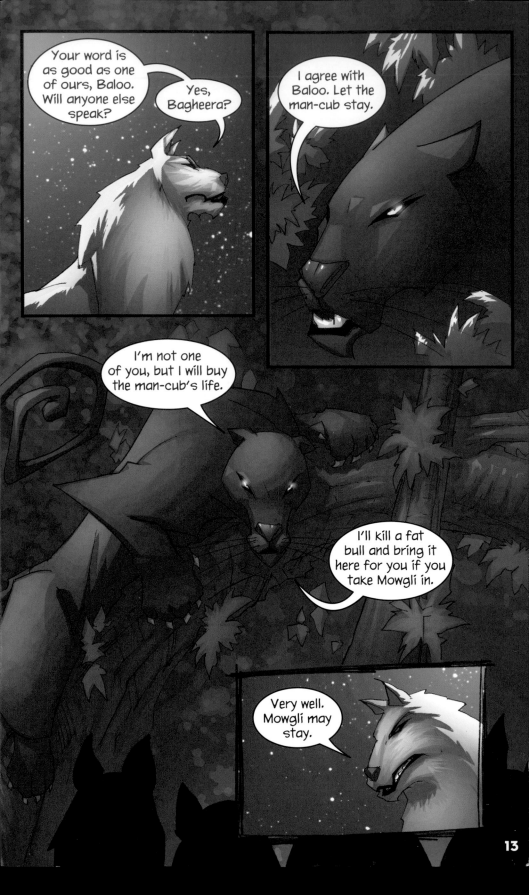

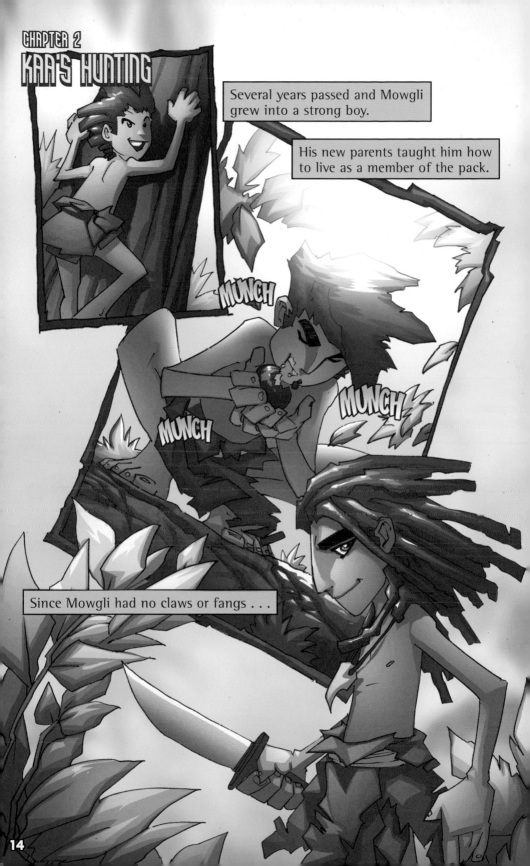

. . . Bagheera taught him how to hunt with a knife instead.

Baloo taught Mowgli and his wolf brothers the laws of the jungle.

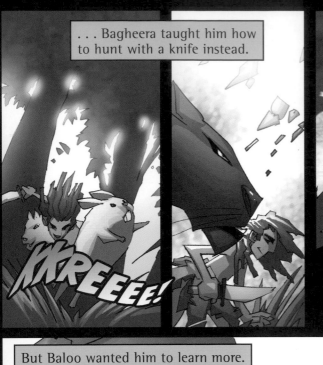

KKREEEE!

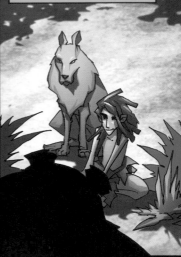

But Baloo wanted him to learn more.

So, he taught Mowgli the laws and customs of all the Jungle Folk . . .

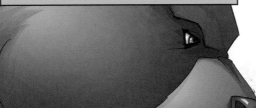

. . . all but one.

Why don't you ever teach me about the monkeys?

I am just like them.

No, you're nothing like them. All they do is lie and show off.

Stay away from them, Mowgli.

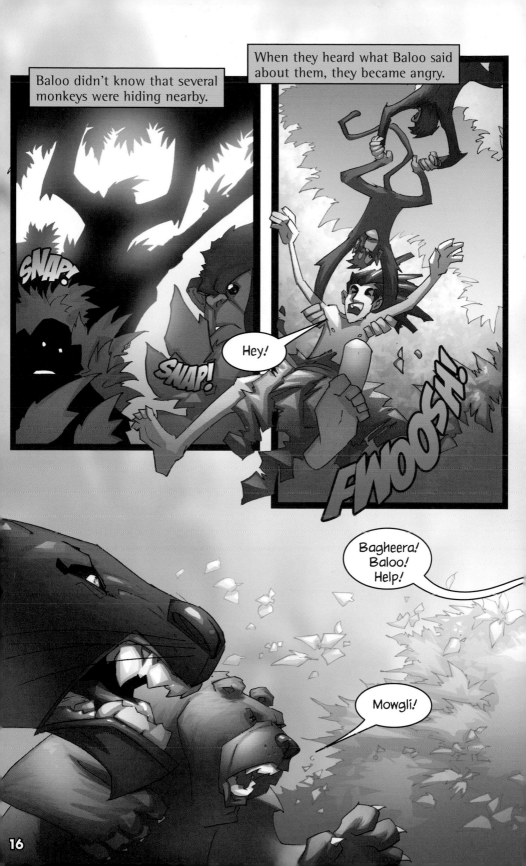

Baloo didn't know that several monkeys were hiding nearby.

When they heard what Baloo said about them, they became angry.

SNAP!

SNAP!

Hey!

FWOOSH!

Bagheera! Baloo! Help!

Mowgli!

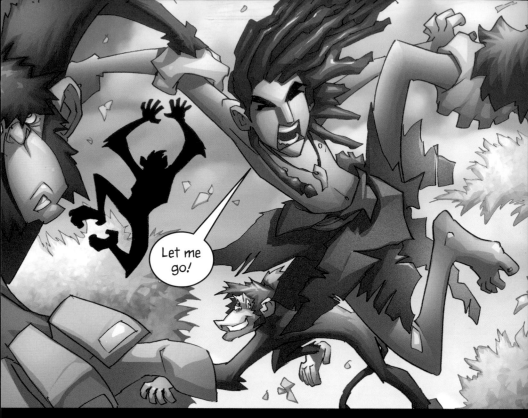

Let me go!

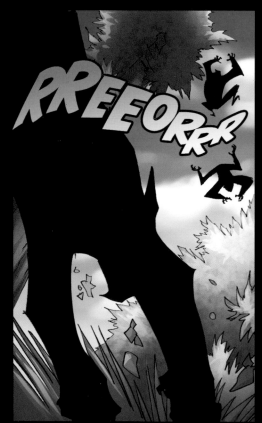

RREEORR

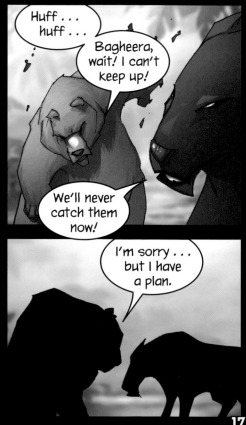

Huff . . . huff . . .

Bagheera, wait! I can't keep up!

We'll never catch them now!

I'm sorry . . . but I have a plan.

The monkeys took Mowgli to a secret place called the Cold Lairs.

It used to be a human city, but the Monkey People lived there now.

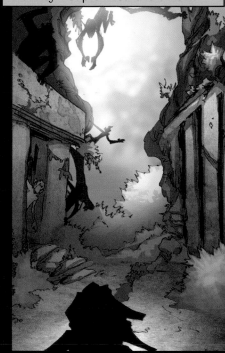

Mowgli was the first human to go there for many years.

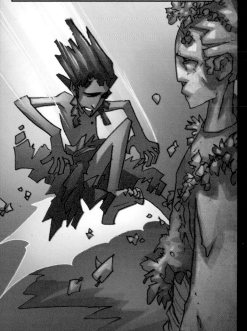

Meanwhile, Baloo and Bagheera paid a visit to an old friend . . .

Hello, Kaa!

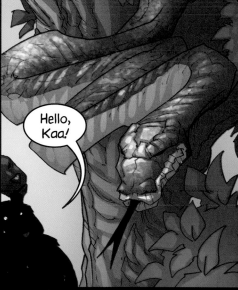

8

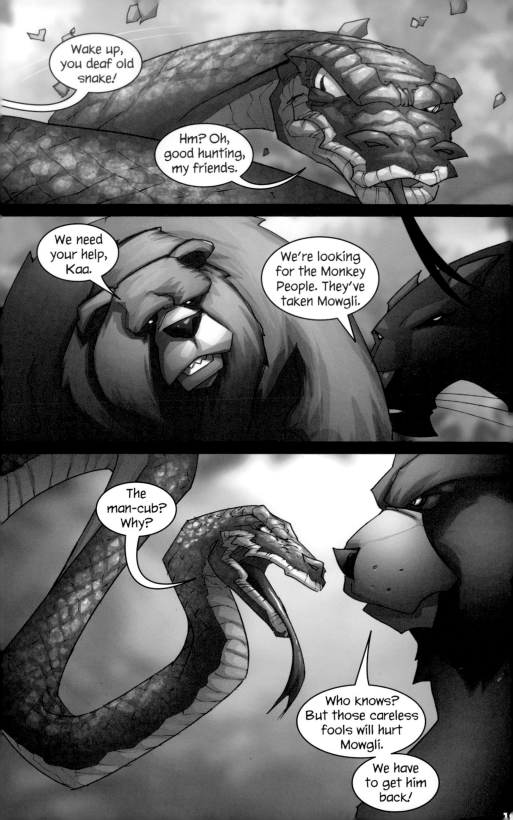

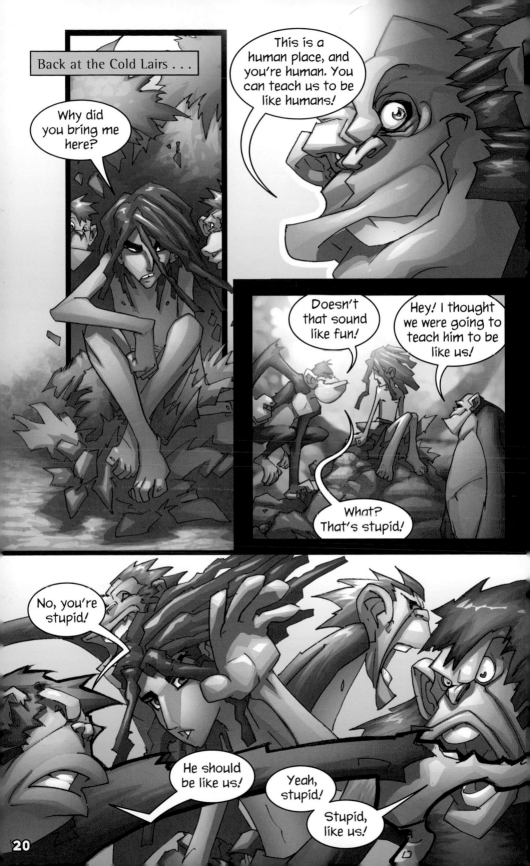

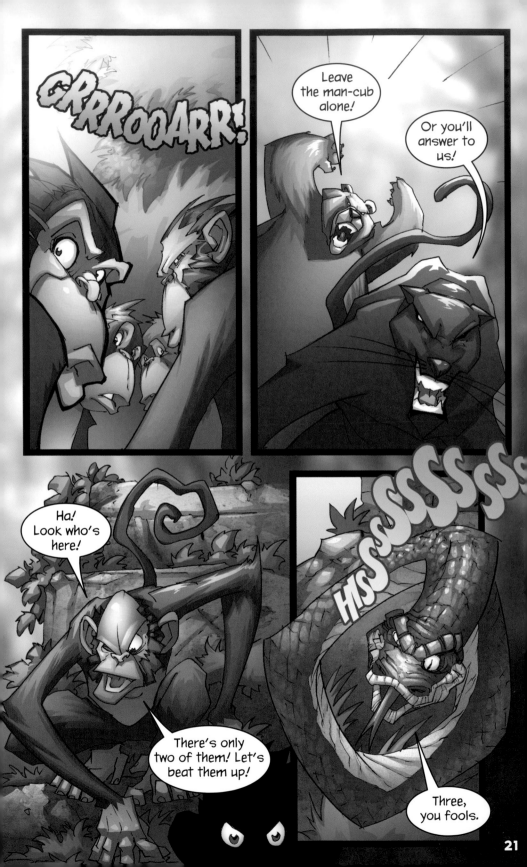

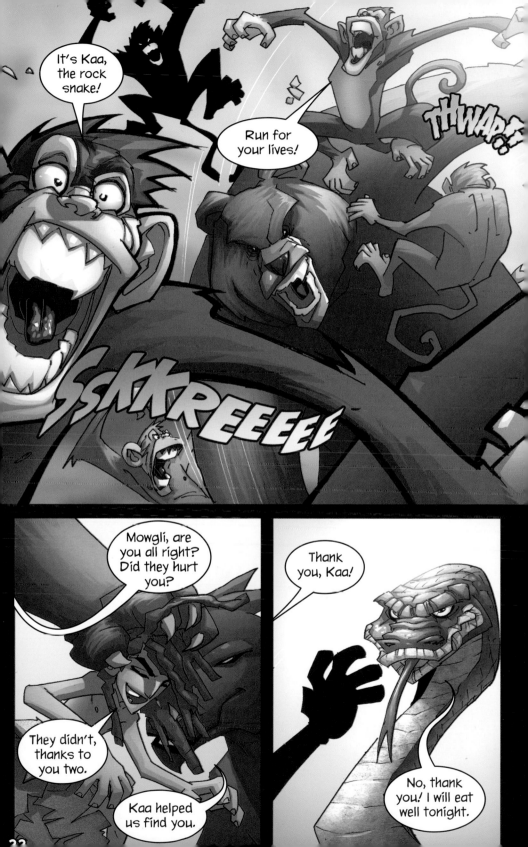

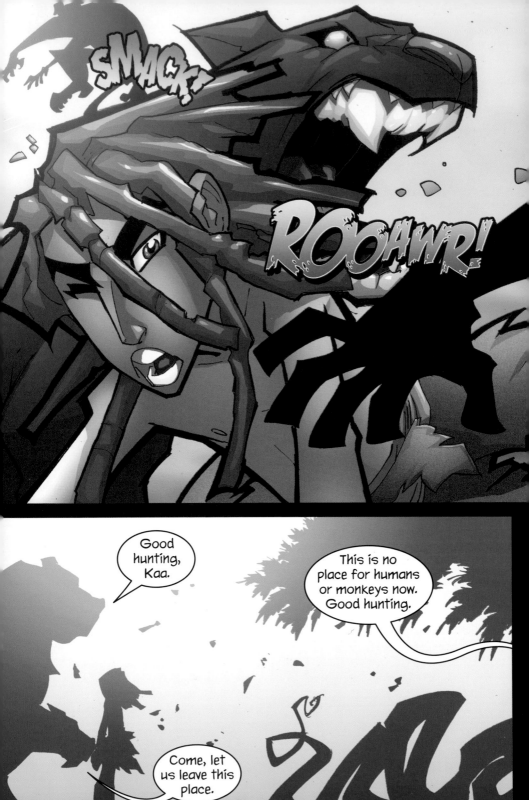

# CHAPTER 3
# THE RED FLOWER

As months passed in the jungle, Mowgli's brothers grew quickly.

In time, Father Wolf died.

Mowgli hunted for his mother, just as Father Wolf had done.

I worry for you, Mowgli. Shere Khan still wants to kill you.

He speaks to the younger wolves sometimes.

He wants to turn them against you.

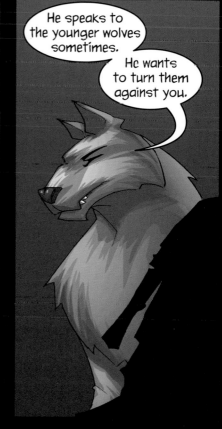

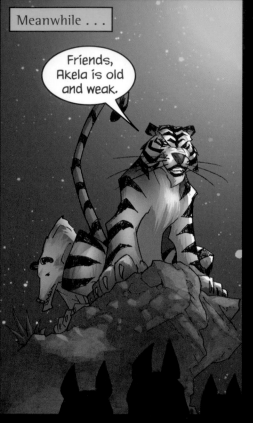

Friends, Akela is old and weak.

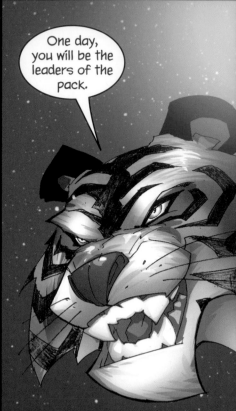

One day, you will be the leaders of the pack.

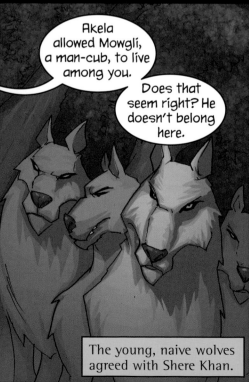

Akela allowed Mowgli, a man-cub, to live among you.

Does that seem right? He doesn't belong here.

The young, naive wolves agreed with Shere Khan.

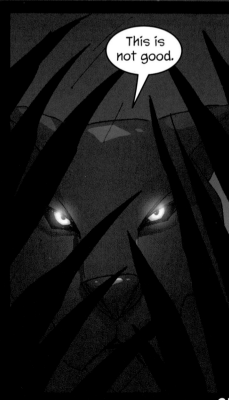

This is not good.

25

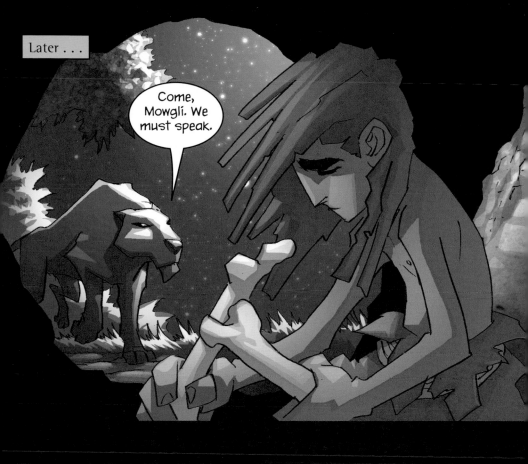

Come, Mowgli. We must speak.

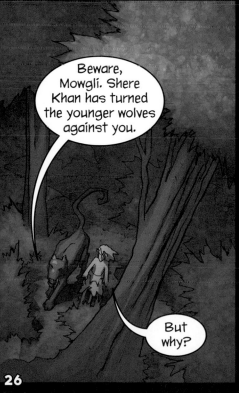

Beware, Mowgli. Shere Khan has turned the younger wolves against you.

But why?

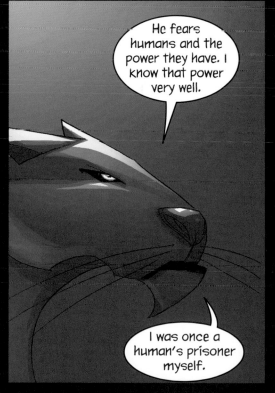

He fears humans and the power they have. I know that power very well.

I was once a human's prisoner myself.

26

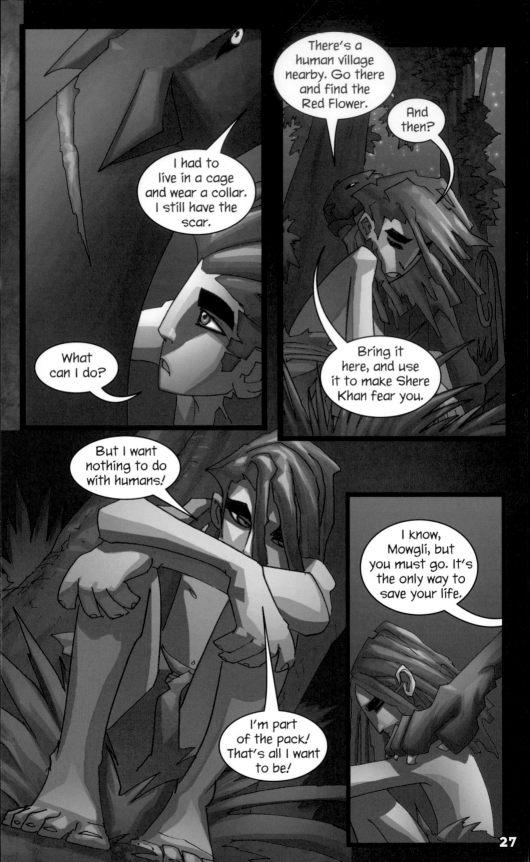

There's a human village nearby. Go there and find the Red Flower.

And then?

I had to live in a cage and wear a collar. I still have the scar.

What can I do?

Bring it here, and use it to make Shere Khan fear you.

But I want nothing to do with humans!

I know, Mowgli, but you must go. It's the only way to save your life.

I'm part of the pack! That's all I want to be!

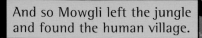

And so Mowgli left the jungle and found the human village.

He saw a girl carrying something that smelled like the Red Flower.

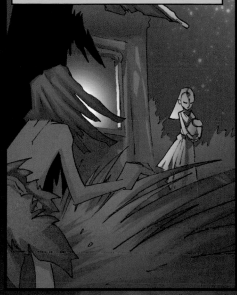

Frightened by Mowgli, the girl dropped what she was carrying and ran away.

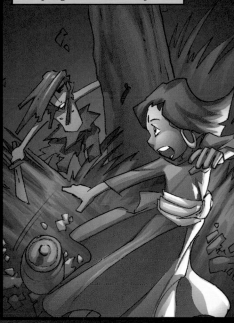

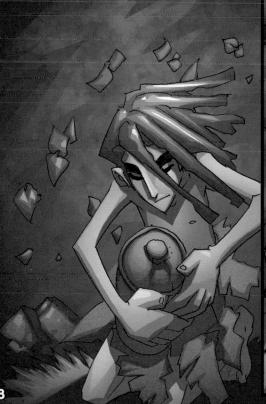

Within, Mowgli found a seed of the Red Flower.

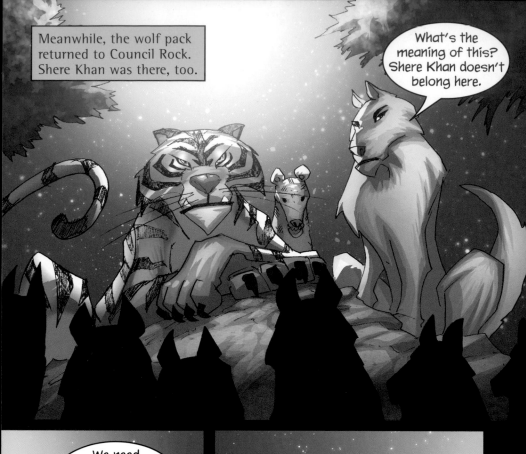

Meanwhile, the wolf pack returned to Council Rock. Shere Khan was there, too.

What's the meaning of this? Shere Khan doesn't belong here.

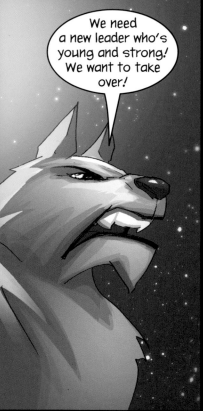

We need a new leader who's young and strong! We want to take over!

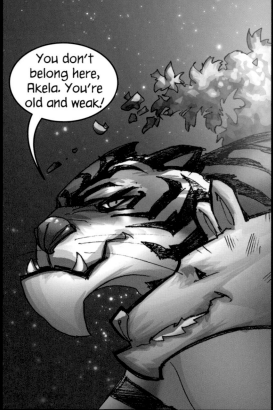

You don't belong here, Akela. You're old and weak!

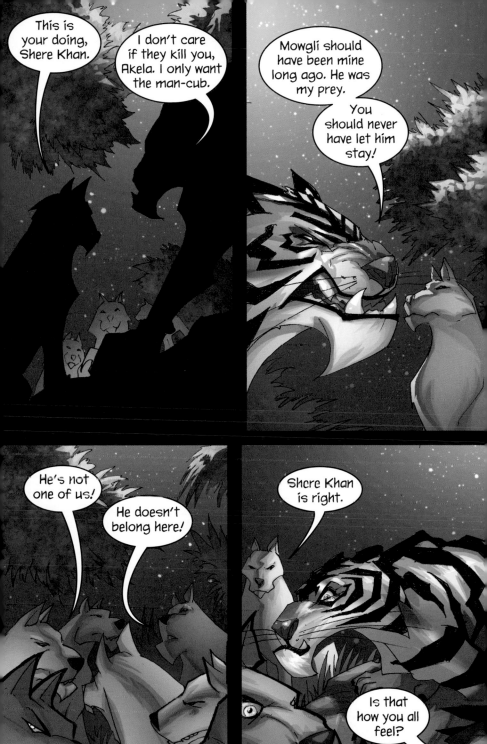

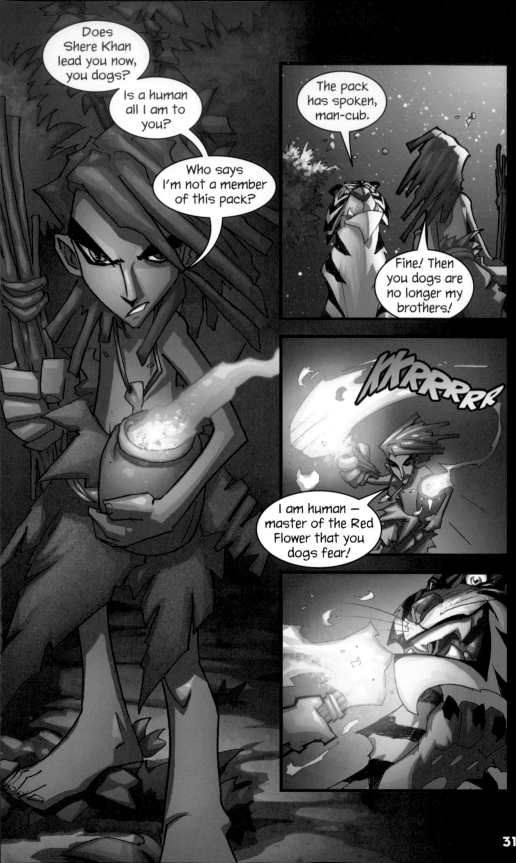

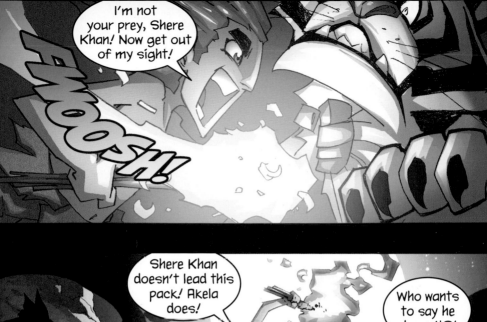

I'm not your prey, Shere Khan! Now get out of my sight!

FWOOSH!

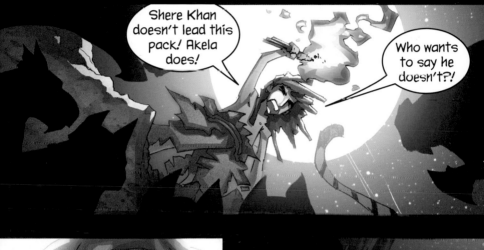

Shere Khan doesn't lead this pack! Akela does!

Who wants to say he doesn't?!

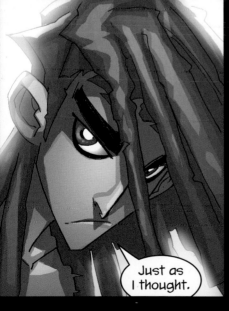

Just as I thought.

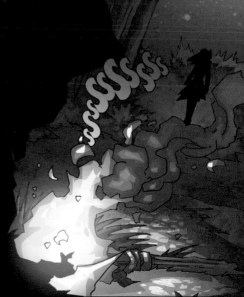

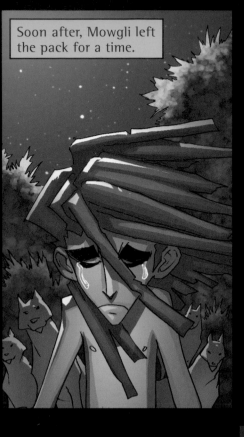

Soon after, Mowgli left the pack for a time.

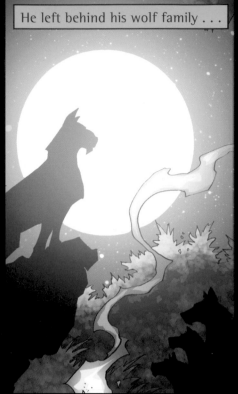

He left behind his wolf family . . .

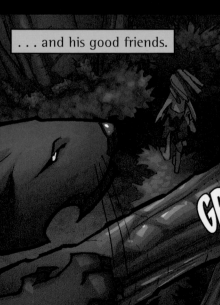

. . . and his good friends.

He also left behind a fearsome enemy.

One more determined than ever to kill him.

GRRRRRRR

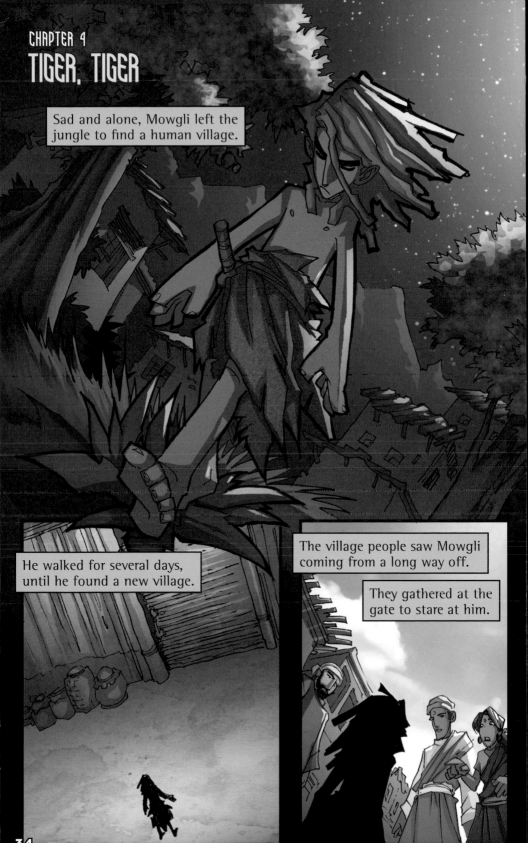

One of the them, a woman named Messua, thought she recognized the young boy.

Messua once lived closer to the jungle. A tiger had killed her husband. She thought that tiger had also killed Nathoo, her son.

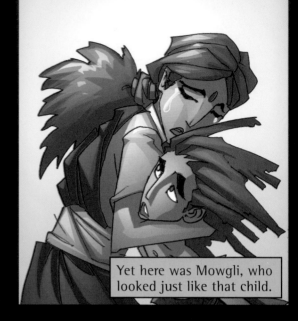

Nathoo . . . ?

Yet here was Mowgli, who looked just like that child.

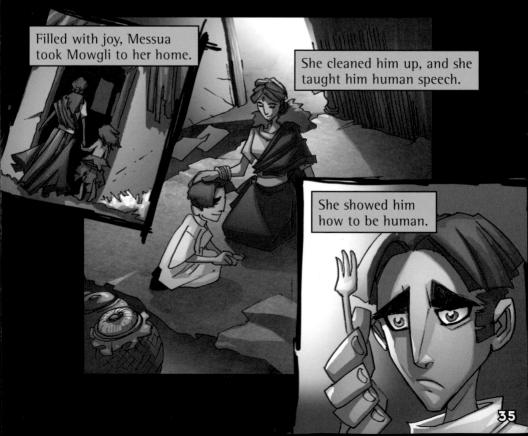

Filled with joy, Messua took Mowgli to her home.

She cleaned him up, and she taught him human speech.

She showed him how to be human.

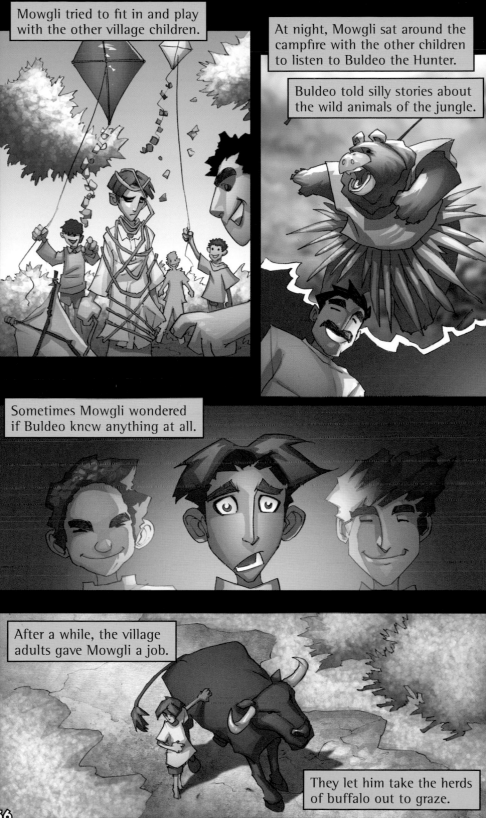

One day, two old friends came to visit . . .

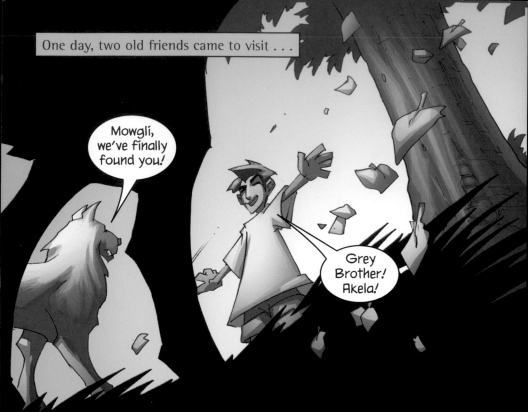

Mowgli, we've finally found you!

Grey Brother! Akela!

The entire pack, especially these two, had missed Mowgli.

They were glad to find him, for they had news to share.

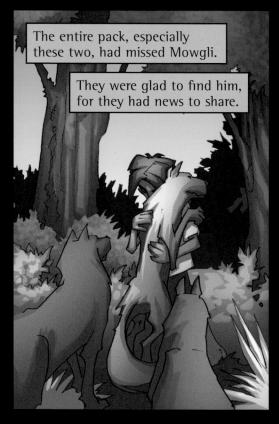

Shere Khan has not forgotten you, Mowgli. He still wants to kill you.

He's been hunting you. He knows you live here.

He's hiding near the river, waiting for nightfall.

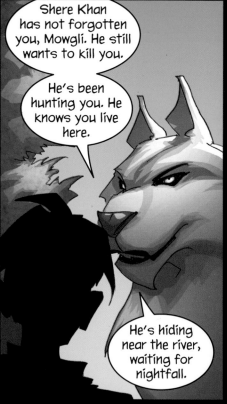

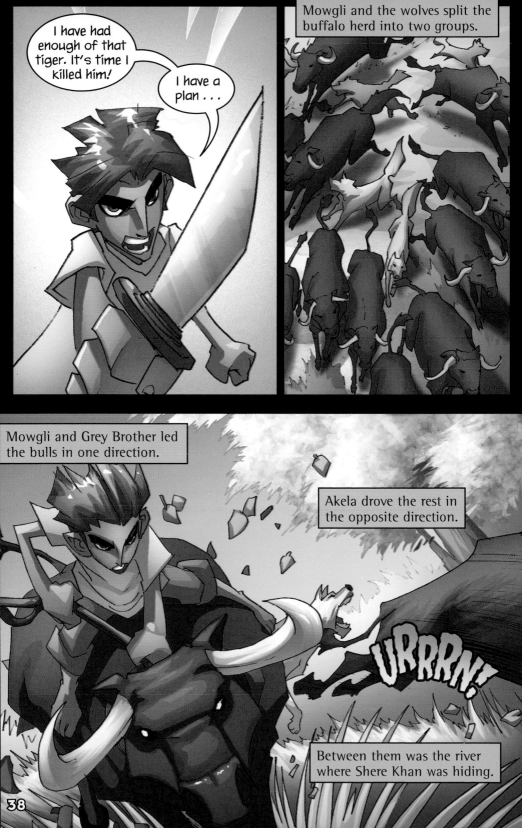

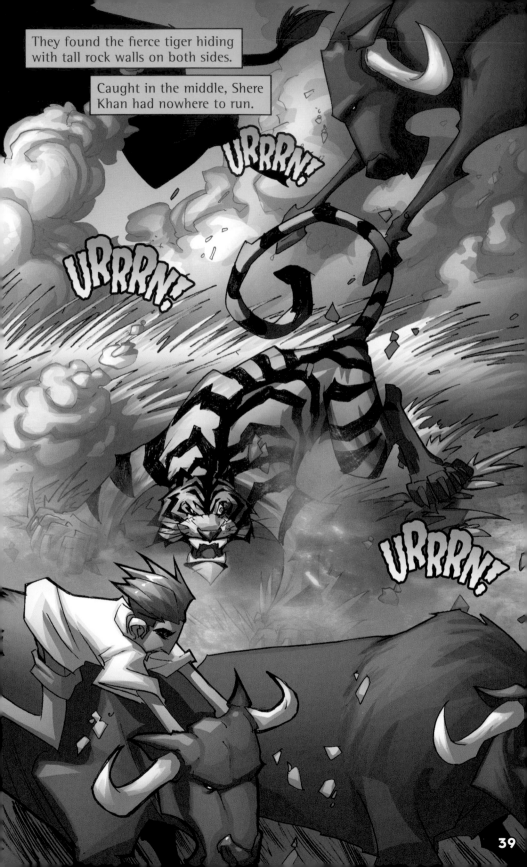

When it was over, Shere Khan lay trampled, dead.

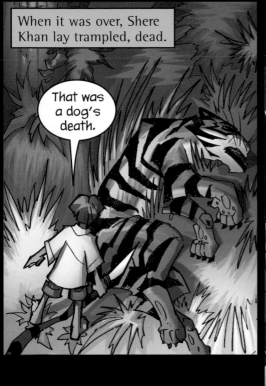

That was a dog's death.

Right away, Mowgli began to skin Shere Khan's hide.

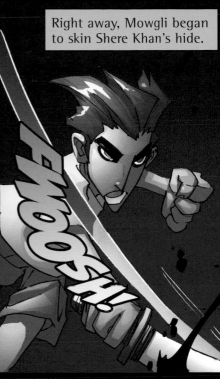

FWOOSH!

Meanwhile, Buldeo the Hunter came looking for Mowgli . . .

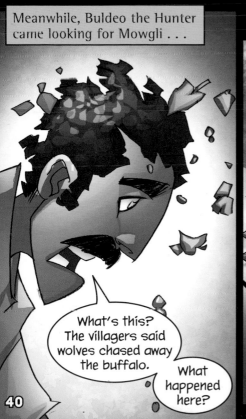

What's this? The villagers said wolves chased away the buffalo.

What happened here?

Mowgli told Buldeo the story, which frightened the hunter.

I'm going to tell the villagers about this!

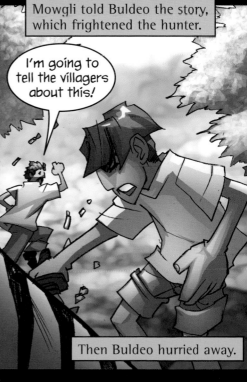

Then Buldeo hurried away.

When Mowgli returned to the village, he found all the villagers waiting for him outside the gate.

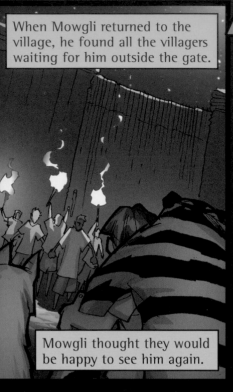

Mowgli thought they would be happy to see him again.

But . . .

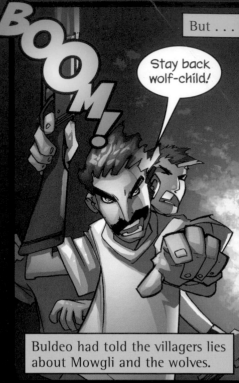

Stay back wolf-child!

BOOM!

Buldeo had told the villagers lies about Mowgli and the wolves.

They didn't want Mowgli to live with them anymore.

They shouted and threw stones.

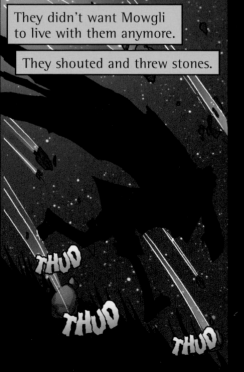

THUD

THUD

THUD

Only one person supported Mowgli. Messua didn't believe Buldeo's story.

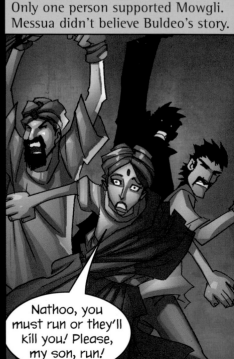

Nathoo, you must run or they'll kill you! Please, my son, run!

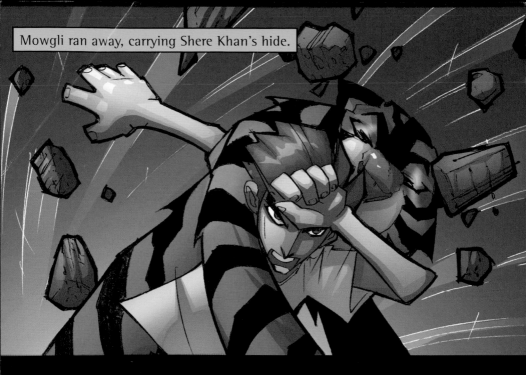

Mowgli ran away, carrying Shere Khan's hide.

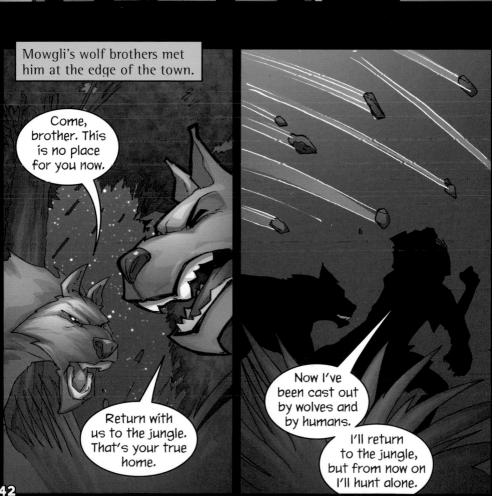

Mowgli's wolf brothers met him at the edge of the town.

Come, brother. This is no place for you now.

Return with us to the jungle. That's your true home.

Now I've been cast out by wolves and by humans.

I'll return to the jungle, but from now on I'll hunt alone.

42

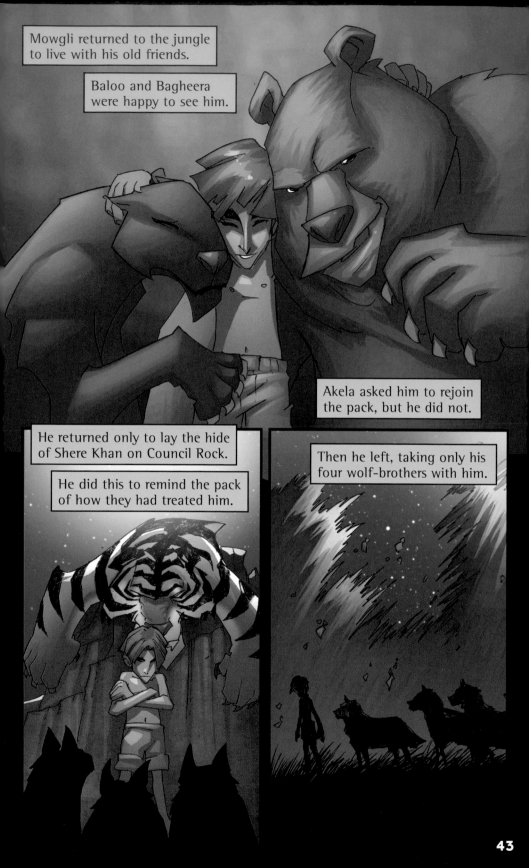

Mowgli returned to the jungle to live with his old friends.

Baloo and Bagheera were happy to see him.

Akela asked him to rejoin the pack, but he did not.

He returned only to lay the hide of Shere Khan on Council Rock.

He did this to remind the pack of how they had treated him.

Then he left, taking only his four wolf-brothers with him.

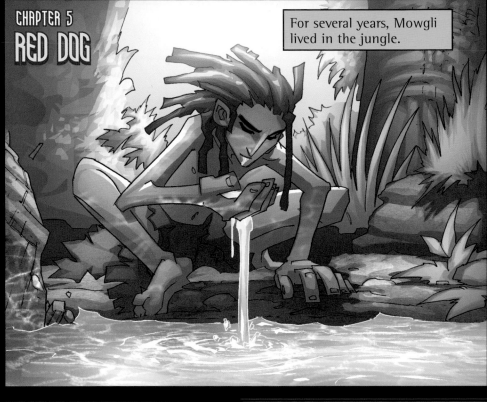

## CHAPTER 5
# RED DOG

For several years, Mowgli lived in the jungle.

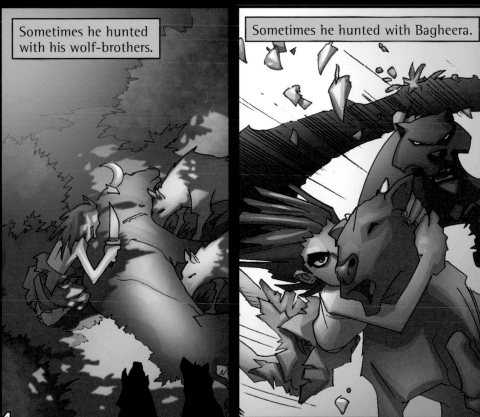

Sometimes he hunted with his wolf-brothers.

Sometimes he hunted with Bagheera.

At other times, he helped Baloo teach new cubs the laws of the jungle.

In time, Mother Wolf grew old and died. Mowgli rolled a stone over the mouth of her den.

He would never go back there again.

In the years that followed, Mowgli had many adventures.

He grew to be a strong young man.

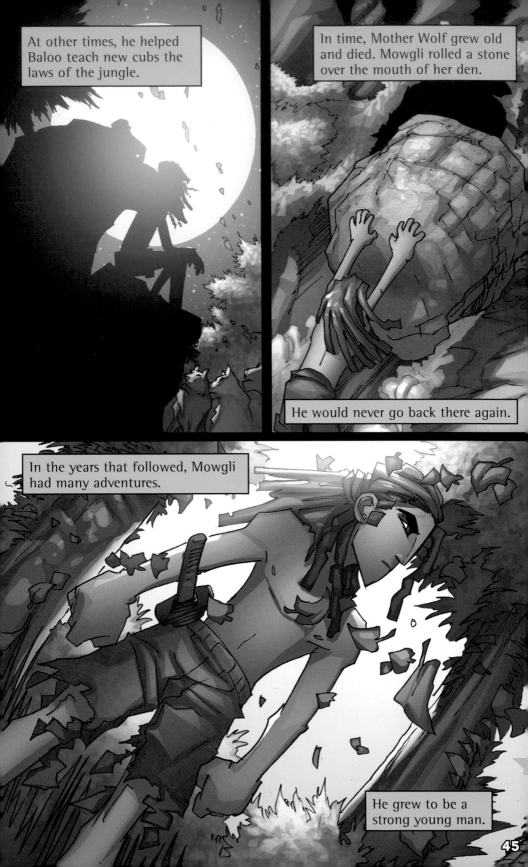

For a while, nothing changed but the seasons.

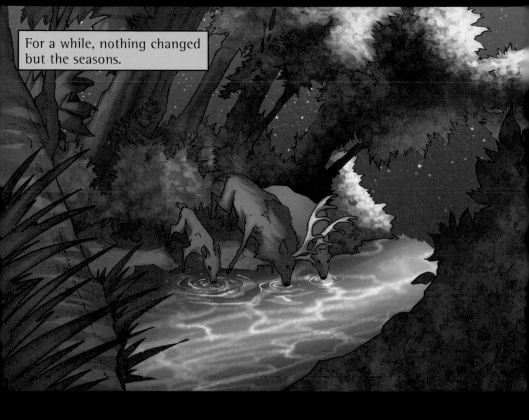

Then one night, a terrible shriek rang out.

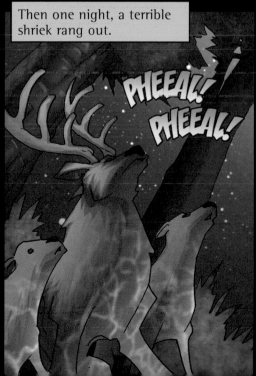

The cry was the pheeal. It served as a warning to the Jungle Folk.

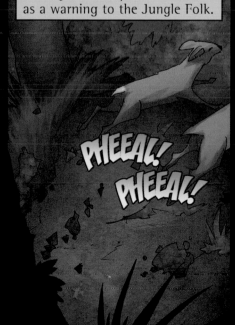

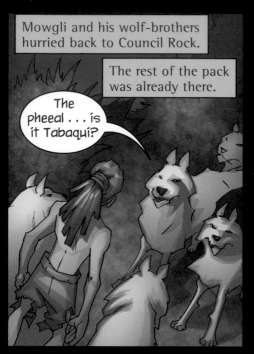

Mowgli and his wolf-brothers hurried back to Council Rock.

The rest of the pack was already there.

The pheeal . . . is it Tabaqui?

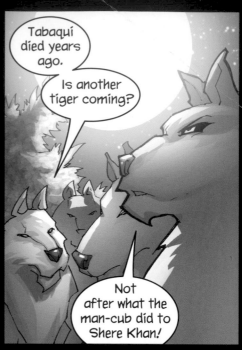

Tabaqui died years ago.

Is another tiger coming?

Not after what the man-cub did to Shere Khan!

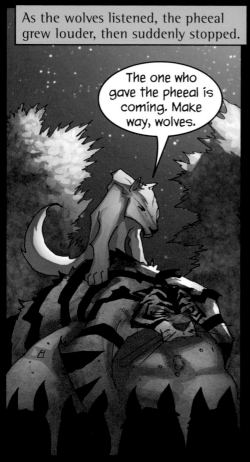

As the wolves listened, the pheeal grew louder, then suddenly stopped.

The one who gave the pheeal is coming. Make way, wolves.

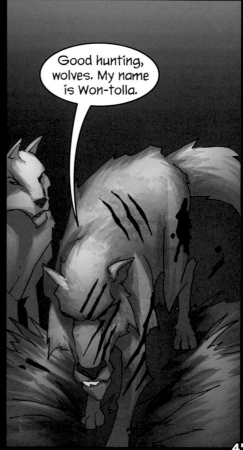

Good hunting, wolves. My name is Won-tolla.

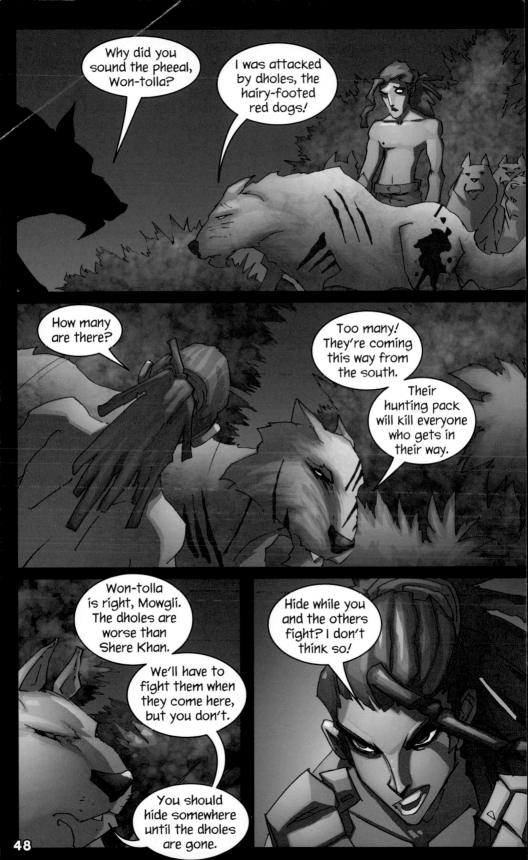

48

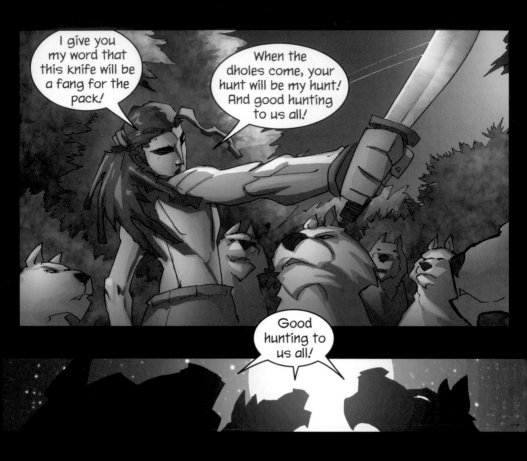

I give you my word that this knife will be a fang for the pack!

When the dholes come, your hunt will be my hunt! And good hunting to us all!

Good hunting to us all!

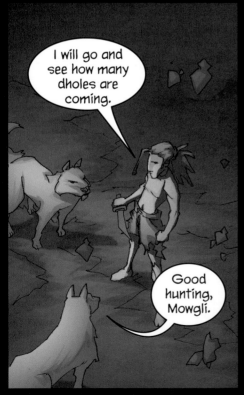

I will go and see how many dholes are coming.

Good hunting, Mowgli.

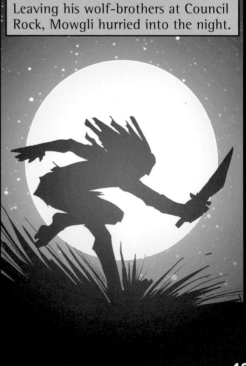

Leaving his wolf-brothers at Council Rock, Mowgli hurried into the night.

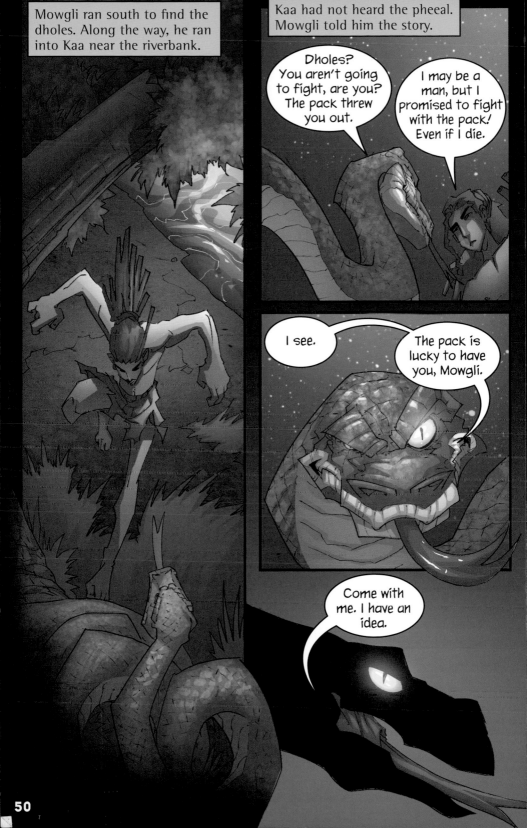

Mowgli ran south to find the dholes. Along the way, he ran into Kaa near the riverbank.

Kaa had not heard the pheeal. Mowgli told him the story.

Dholes? You aren't going to fight, are you? The pack threw you out.

I may be a man, but I promised to fight with the pack! Even if I die.

I see.

The pack is lucky to have you, Mowgli.

Come with me. I have an idea.

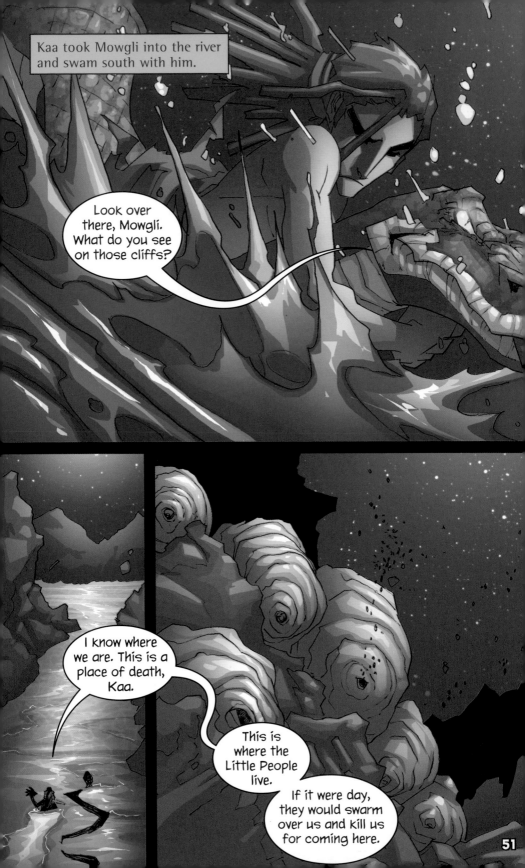

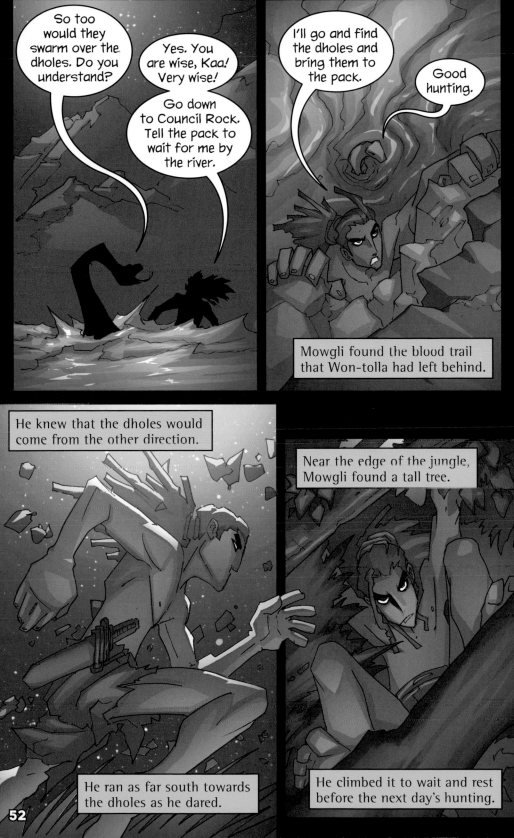

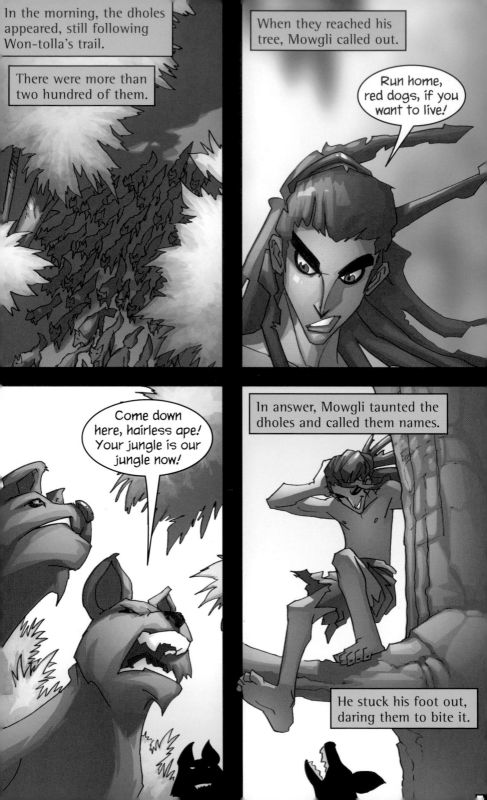

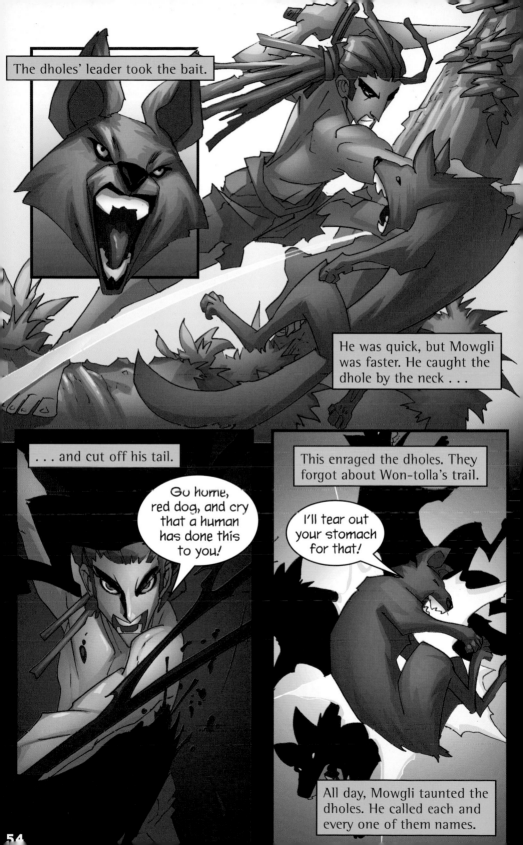

The dholes' leader took the bait.

He was quick, but Mowgli was faster. He caught the dhole by the neck . . .

. . . and cut off his tail.

Go home, red dog, and cry that a human has done this to you!

This enraged the dholes. They forgot about Won-tolla's trail.

I'll tear out your stomach for that!

All day, Mowgli taunted the dholes. He called each and every one of them names.

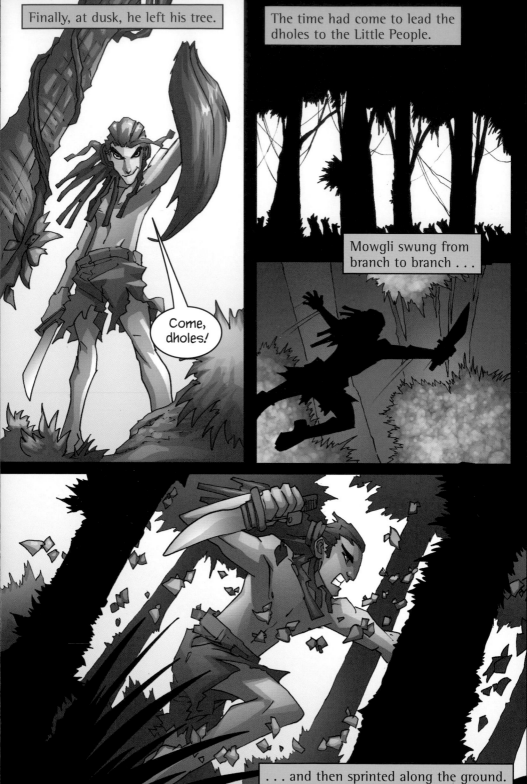

Finally, at dusk, he left his tree.

The time had come to lead the dholes to the Little People.

Come, dholes!

Mowgli swung from branch to branch . . .

. . . and then sprinted along the ground.

He led the dholes north through the jungle and towards the cliffs.

Below was the river, and the homes of the Little People.

At the cliffs' edge, Mowgli jumped, knocking down several stones.

These stones fell on the homes of the Little People, angering them.

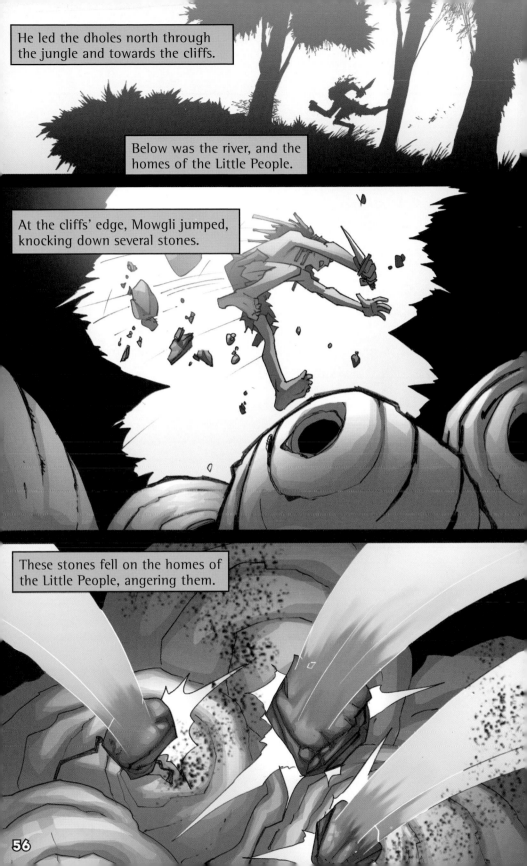

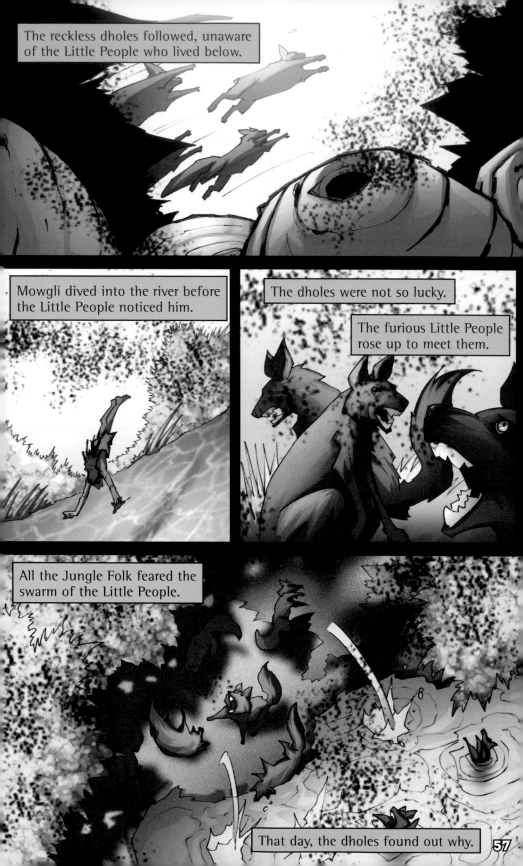

The reckless dholes followed, unaware of the Little People who lived below.

Mowgli dived into the river before the Little People noticed him.

The dholes were not so lucky.

The furious Little People rose up to meet them.

All the Jungle Folk feared the swarm of the Little People.

That day, the dholes found out why.

The Little People killed many dholes.

Good hunting, Little People!

But the hunt was not yet finished. Mowgli swam as fast as he could.

He was tired from his long run, so he could not swim far.

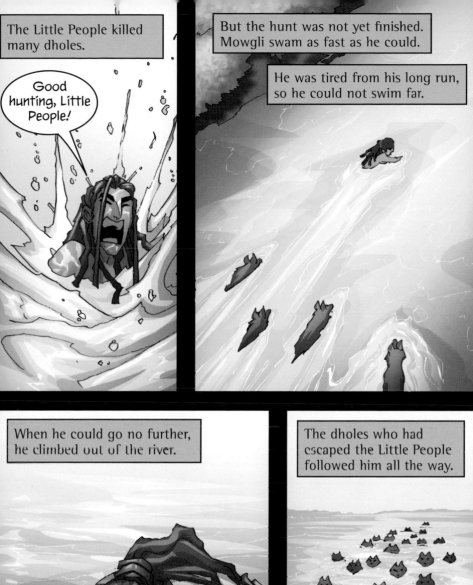

When he could go no further, he climbed out of the river.

The dholes who had escaped the Little People followed him all the way.

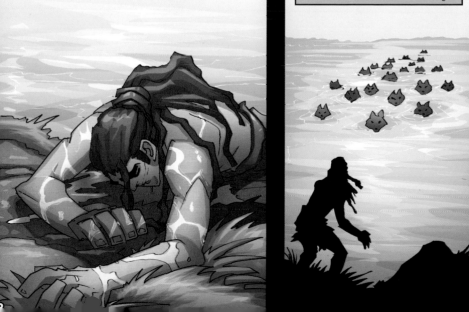

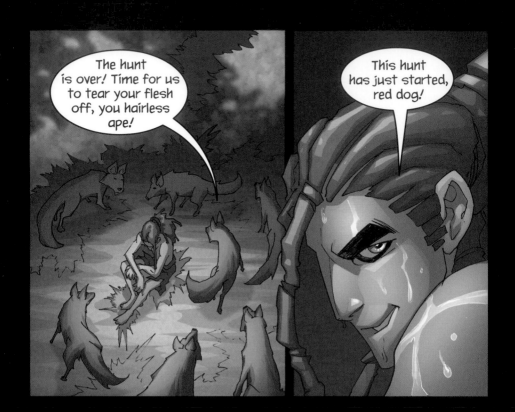

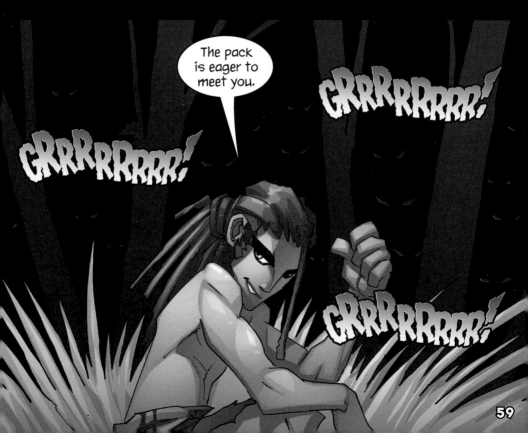

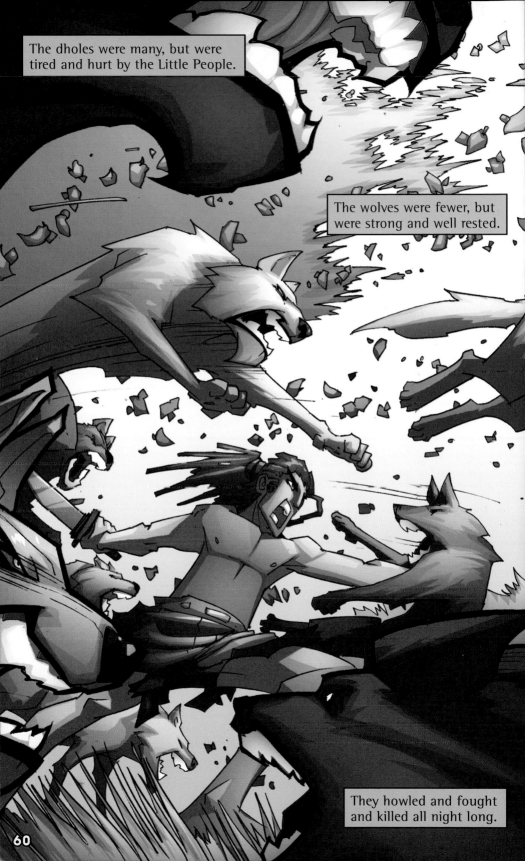

The dholes were many, but were tired and hurt by the Little People.

The wolves were fewer, but were strong and well rested.

They howled and fought and killed all night long.

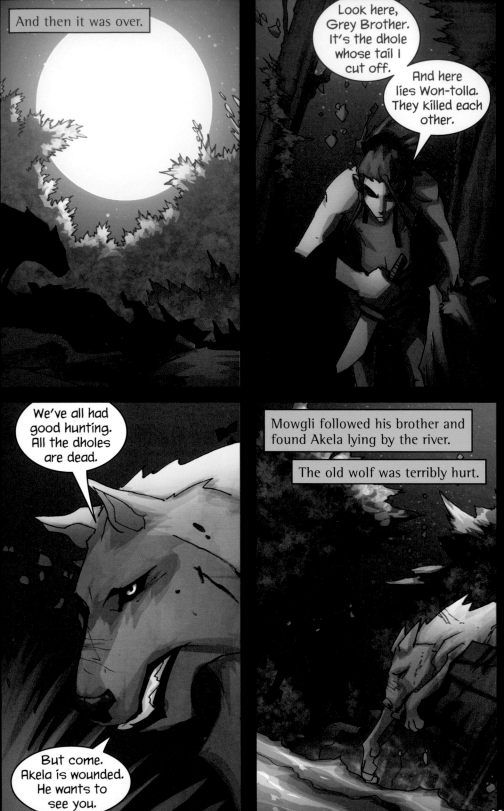

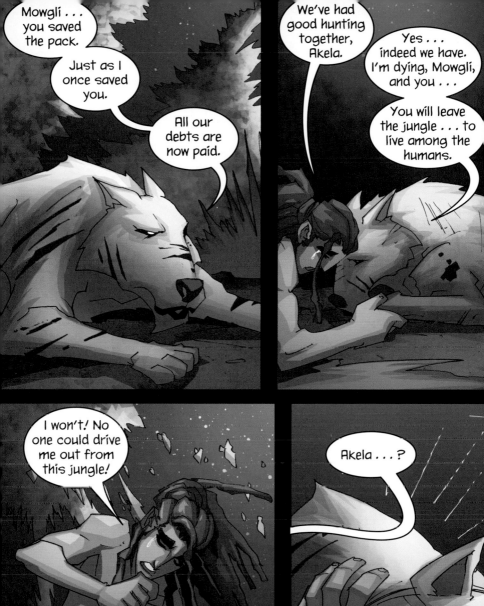
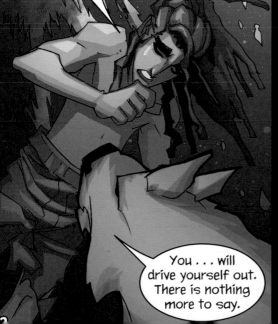
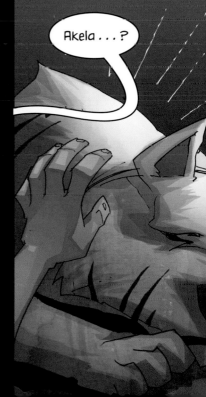

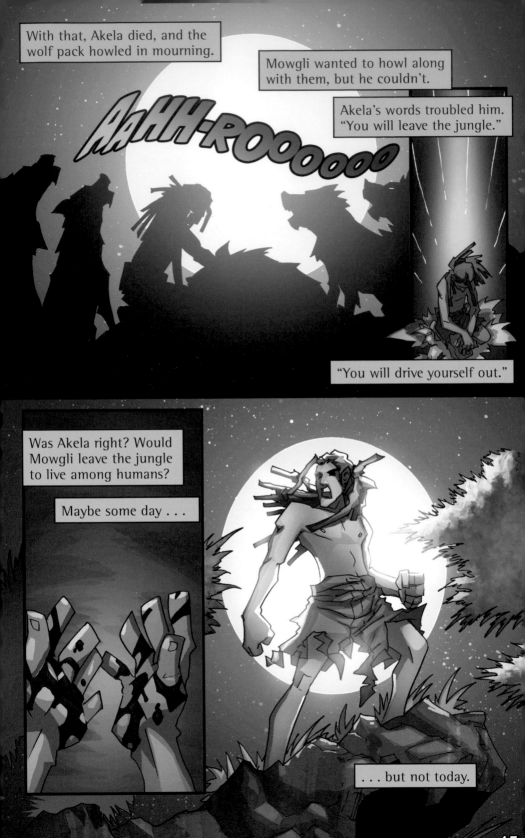

With that, Akela died, and the wolf pack howled in mourning.

Mowgli wanted to howl along with them, but he couldn't.

Akela's words troubled him. "You will leave the jungle."

AaHH-ROOOOOO

"You will drive yourself out."

Was Akela right? Would Mowgli leave the jungle to live among humans?

Maybe some day . . .

. . . but not today.

# LAW OF THE JUNGLE

In 1895, a sequel to *The Jungle Book* was published. It was called *The Second Jungle Book*, and it continued the stories of Mowgli and his friends.

This book contains a poem called "The Law of the Jungle," which outlines a code of conduct and behaviour for the Jungle Folk. Baloo would sing the poem to the wolf cubs to teach them the ways of the pack.

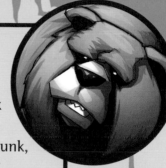

Now this is the Law of the Jungle — as old and as true as the sky;

And the Wolf that shall keep it may prosper, but the Wolf that shall break it must die.

As the creeper that girdles the tree-trunk, the Law runneth forward and back —

For the strength of the Pack is the Wolf, and the strength of the Wolf is the Pack.

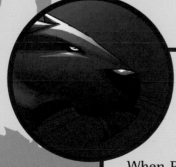

Keep peace with the Lords of the Jungle — the Tiger, the Panther, and Bear.

And trouble not Hathi the Silent, and mock not the Boar in his lair.

When Pack meets with Pack in the Jungle, and neither will go from the trail,

Lie down till the leaders have spoken — it may be fair words shall prevail.

The Lair of the Wolf is his refuge, and where he has made it is home

Not even the Head Wolf may enter, not even the Council may come.

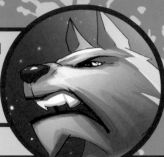

You may kill for yourselves and your mates, and your cubs as they need and you can;

But kill not for pleasure of killing, and seven times never kill Man!

The Kill of the Pack is the meat of the Pack. You must eat where it lies;

And no one may carry away of that meat to his lair, or he dies.

The Kill of the Wolf is the meat of the Wolf. He may do what he will;

But, till he has given permission, the Pack may not eat of that Kill.

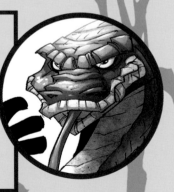

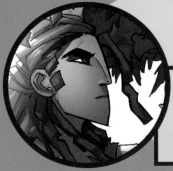

Now these are the Laws of the Jungle, and many and mighty are they;

But the head and hoof of the Law and the haunch and the hump is — OBEY!

# ABOUT THE AUTHOR
# AND ILLUSTRATOR

## ABOUT THE AUTHOR

Joseph Rudyard Kipling was born in Bombay, India, on
30 December 1865. He is best known for his collection of
stories called *The Jungle Book*, which was published in 1894.
He wrote lots of other short stories, including "Kim" and "The
Man Who Would Be King," as well as many poems. In 1907,
he received the Nobel Prize in Literature, becoming both the
first English-language writer and the youngest person to win
the award. He died in London on 18 January 1936, aged 70.

## ABOUT THE RETELLING AUTHOR

Carl Bowen is a writer and editor. He has published a handful
of novels and more than a dozen short stories, all while
working as an advertising copywriter and an editor at White
Wolf Publishing. His first graphic novel is called *Exalted*.

## ABOUT THE ILLUSTRATOR

Gerardo Sandoval is a professional comic book illustrator from
Mexico. He has worked on many well-known comics including
Tomb Raider books from Top Cow Production. He has also
worked on designs for posters and card sets.

# GLOSSARY

**beware** warning to look out for something dangerous or harmful

**careless** someone who is careless does not think things through and often makes mistakes

**dared** was brave enough to do something

**den** home of a wild animal

**determined** if you are determined to do something, you have made a firm decision to do it

**enraged** made someone very angry

**herd** large group of animals that moves together as a group

**mourning** being very sad and grieving for someone who has died

**pack** group of wolves or other animals that sticks together

**regret** be sad or sorry about something

**taunted** tried to make someone angry or upset by teasing them

**trampled** damaged or crushed something by walking over it

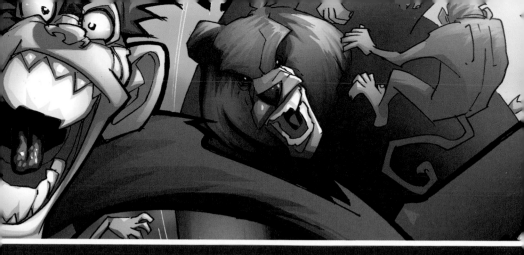

# DISCUSSION QUESTIONS

1. Mowgli tricked the dholes into being attacked by the Little People. Is it ever okay to trick others? Why or why not?

2. Do you think it's possible for a human baby to be raised by wild animals? Explain your answer.

3. Should Mowgli return to live with humans, or does he belong in the jungle with the pack? If you were him, which would you choose?

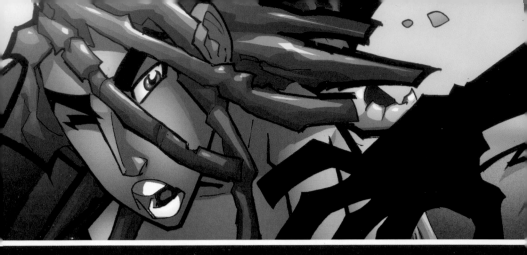

# WRITING PROMPTS

1. When Mowgli was young, Baloo taught him many things. Which person in your life has taught you the most? What did he or she teach you? Write about it.

2. There are many interesting characters in this book. Choose your favourite character and retell your favourite part of this story from that character's perspective.

3. At the end of the book, Mowgli has not yet decided if he will stay with the pack or return to live with humans. Write a final chapter to Mowgli's story about what he does next.

# OTHER BOOKS

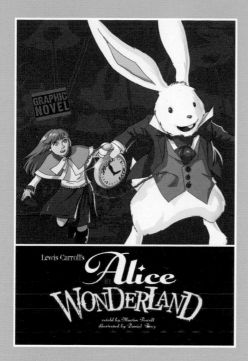

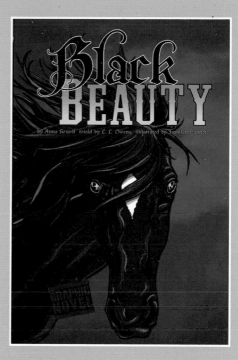

## ALICE IN WONDERLAND

One day, a young girl named Alice spots a frantic White Rabbit wearing a waistcoat and carrying a pocket watch. She follows the hurrying creature down a hole into the magical world of Wonderland. While there, Alice meets more crazy creatures, and plays a twisted game of croquet with the Queen of Hearts. But when the Queen turns against her, this dream-like world quickly becomes a nightmare.

## BLACK BEAUTY

A handsome colt named Black Beauty has a happy childhood growing up in the peaceful countryside. In his later years, he encounters terrible illness and a frightening stable fire. Things go from bad to worse when Black Beauty's new owners begin renting him out for profit. Black Beauty endures a life of mistreatment and disrespect in a world that shows little regard for the wellbeing of animals.

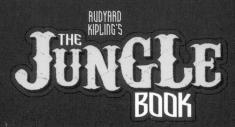

# RUDYARD KIPLING'S
# THE JUNGLE BOOK

**www.raintreepublishers.co.uk**
Visit our website to find out
more information about
Raintree books.

Phone 0845 6044371
Fax +44 (0) 1865 312263
Email myorders@capstonepub.co.uk

Customers from outside the UK please telephone +44 1865 312262

Raintree is an imprint of Capstone Global Library Limited, a company incorporated in
England and Wales having its registered office at 7 Pilgrim Street, London, EC4V 6LB –
Registered company number: 6695582

"Raintree" is a registered trademark of Pearson Education Limited, under licence to
Capstone Global Library Limited

Art Director: Bob Lentz
Designer: Brann Garvey
Creative Director: Heather Kindseth
Editorial Director: Michael Dahl
Editor: Donald Lemke
Associate Editor: Sean Tulien
UK Editor: Laura Knowles
Originated by Capstone Global Library Ltd
Printed and bound in China by Leo Paper Products Ltd

ISBN 978 1 406214 15 4 (hardback)
14 13 12 11 10
10 9 8 7 6 5 4 3 2 1

ISBN 978 1 406214 19 2 (paperback)
14 13 12 11 10
10 9 8 7 6 5 4 3 2 1

**British Library Cataloguing in Publication Data**
A full catalogue record for this book is available from the British Library.

RUDYARD KIPLING'S

# THE JUNGLE BOOK

RETOLD BY CARL BOWEN
ILLUSTRATED BY GERARDO SANDOVAL
COLOURED BY BENNY FUENTES

**Raintree**